DARK MAN

ESCAPE FROM THE DARK

BY
PETER LANCETT

ILLUSTRATED BY JAN PEDROIETTA

Librarian Reviewer
Laurie K. Holland
Media Specialist (National Board Certified), Edina, MN
MA in Elementary Education, Minnesota State University, Mankato

Reading Consultant
Elizabeth Stedem
Educator/Consultant, Colorado Springs, CO
MA in Elementary Education, University of Denver, CO

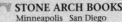
STONE ARCH BOOKS
Minneapolis   San Diego

First published in the United States in 2008
by Stone Arch Books
151 Good Counsel Drive, P.O. Box 669
Mankato, Minnesota 56002
www.stonearchbooks.com

Library of Congress Cataloging-in-Publication Data
Lancett, Peter.
    Escape from the Dark / by Peter Lancett; illustrated by
Jan Pedroietta.
    p. cm. — (Zone Books. Dark Man)
    Summary: A frightened and sick girl visits the Dark Man,
bringing him an important note, and as they leave his dirty room,
she is no longer ill.
    ISBN-13: 978-1-59889-867-5 (library binding)
    ISBN-10: 1-59889-867-1 (library binding)
    ISBN-13: 978-1-59889-927-6 (paperback)
    ISBN-10: 1-59889-927-9 (paperback)
    [1. Good and evil—Fiction.] I. Pedroietta, Jan, ill. II. Title.
PZ7.L2313Es 2008
[Fic]—dc22   2007003965

Art Director: Heather Kindseth
Graphic Designer: Kay Fraser

Photo Credits
Photo Disc, 20; Rubberball Visuality, cover, 4, 16, 17, 22, 25, 28, 33

1 2 3 4 5 6 12 11 10 09 08 07

Printed in the United States of America

TABLE OF CONTENTS

In the dark and distant future, the Shadow Masters control the night. These evil powers threaten to cover the earth in complete darkness. One man has the power to stop them. He is the Dark Man — the world's only light of hope.

(CHAPTER ONE)

THE GIRL

It is night.

The room is **dark**. The room
is **dirty**.

The windows are broken.

The room is **quiet**.

A man sits on the floor. It is the Dark Man.

His back rests against a wall.

The man looks up.

He hears the wooden stairs **creak**.

The door opens.

A **girl** stands in the doorway.

She sees the man and is afraid.

"Come in," he says.

The girl does **not** move.

❨ CHAPTER TWO ❩

THE NOTE

"Do not be **afraid**," the man says.

The girl takes **one** step into the room.

"Is it <u>**you**</u>?" the girl asks.

Her voice is **shaky**. She finds it hard to breathe.

"It is," the man says.

Slowly the girl walks over to him.

The man sees that she walks with a **limp**.

The girl holds out her **hand**.

In her hand is a note.

He takes the note.

His fingers **touch** the girl's fingers.

Inside his head there is a **flash of light**.

In a moment he sees the girl's illness.

He sees why she walks with a limp.

He sees why she finds it hard to **breathe.**

The girl is **very ill.**

(CHAPTER THREE)

THE ESCAPE

The Dark Man reads the note.

"There is more," the girl says.

"On the way here, there were **men**. I think they were **following me**," she says.

The Dark Man stands. He brushes the **dust** from his coat.

"You still came," he says. "That was very **brave**."

"The man who gave me the note said that it was important," says the girl. They hear the noise of a door opening.

The Dark Man **takes** the girl's hand.

Her hand feels warm when he
touches it.

"Come," he says. "We must get **out of here**."

They hear **footsteps** on the stairs.

The room has a back door. He leads the girl out of the back door.

They move fast, but they don't
make any **sounds**.

CHAPTER FOUR

THE GIRL ALONE

They step out into the **dark**.

The night is **cold**.

"That was close," he says. "You must go now."

Soon the girl cannot see him.

He is lost in the **shadows**.

Then she notices something.

She does not feel ill.

She can **breathe**, and it is easy to **breathe**.

She begins to walk, and now she can walk fast.

She no longer has a **limp**.

The end . . . for now.

MORE LIGHT ON HEALING BY TOUCH

The Dark Man heals the mystery girl simply by holding her hand. Many people believe touch can have this powerful effect in real life as well.

Scientists believe that touch is a necessary part of life. In fact, studies have shown that babies need hugs, kisses, and other forms of touch in order to survive.

Even ancient people understood the power of touch. The earliest known book about the benefits of massage was written more than 5,000 years ago!

Today, getting a massage is more popular than ever. In fact, more than 20 million Americans get a massage each year.

Reiki (RAY-kee) is a Japanese technique of healing by touch. People who practice Reiki believe that energy can pass through one person's hands into another person's body.

Some believe that touch can cure pain and diseases. During **acupuncture** (AK-yoo-pungk-chur), professionals treat illnesses by poking special needles into the skin.

Chiropractors (KYE-roh-prak-turz) also try to heal their patient's pain or illness with touch. They treat them by adjusting the backbone, also known as the spine.

Human touch isn't the only way to a healthier life. Some scientists believe petting dogs or cats can reduce stress and help a person live longer.

ABOUT THE AUTHOR

Peter Lancett was born in the city of Stoke-on-Trent, England. At age 20, he moved to London. While there, he worked for a film studio and became a partner in a company producing music videos. He later moved to Auckland, New Zealand, where he wrote his first novel, *The Iron Maiden.* Today, Lancett is back in England and continues to write his ghoulish stories.

ABOUT THE ILLUSTRATOR

Jan Pedroietta lives and works in Germany. As a boy, Pedroietta always enjoyed drawing and creating things. He also spent many hours reading his brother's comic books about cowboys and American Indians. Today, comic books still inspire Pedroietta as he continues improving his own skills.

GLOSSARY

creak (KREEK)—a squeaky noise

hope (HOHP)—to expect or wish something would happen

ill (IL)—another word for sick

limp (LIMP)—to walk unevenly because a foot or leg is injured

notices (NOH-tih-sez)—sees or hears or feels something for the first time

power (POU-ur)—great strength and energy, or the ability to do something

Shadow Masters (SHAD-oh MASS-turz)—evil beings that control the darkness in the future. The Shadow Masters want to cover the earth in complete darkness.

shadows (SHAD-ohz)—darkness caused by something blocking the light

DISCUSSION QUESTIONS

1. The Dark Man is the only one who can stop the evil Shadow Masters. But even he needs help. How does the girl help the Dark Man? How does he repay her?

2. The mystery girl gives the Dark Man a note. The reader never learns what this message says. What do you think was on the note?

WRITING PROMPTS

1. The author doesn't reveal the message of the girl's note. Using your imagination, create your own message and write a note to the Dark Man.

2. In the story, the Dark Man and the mystery girl help each other. Think of someone who has helped you in the past. Describe how they helped you and how you thanked them.

INTERNET SITES

Do you want to know more about subjects related to this book? Or are you interested in learning about other topics? Then check out FactHound, a fun, easy way to find Internet sites.

Our investigative staff has already sniffed out great sites for you!

Here's how to use FactHound:

1. Visit *www.facthound.com*

2. Select your grade level.

3. To learn more about subjects related to this book, type in the book's ISBN number: **1598898671**.

4. Click the **Fetch It** button.

FactHound will fetch the best Internet sites for you!